Keira the Film Star Fairy was originally published
as a Rainbow Magic special. This version has
been specially adapted for developing readers
in conjunction with a Reading Consultant.

Special thanks
to Mandy Archer
and Fiona Munro

Reading Consultant: Prue Goodwin, lecturer in literacy and children's books.

ORCHARD BOOKS

This story first published in Great Britain in 2009 by Orchard Books
First published as an Early Reader in 2015

This edition published in 2019 by The Watts Publishing Group

1 3 5 7 9 10 8 6 4 2

HiT entertainment

A CIP catalogue record for this book is available from the British Library.

ISBN 978 1 40835 983 9

Printed in China

MIX
Paper from
responsible sources
FSC® C104740

The paper and board used in this book are made from wood from responsible sources

Orchard Books
An imprint of Hachette Children's Group
Part of The Watts Publishing Group Limited
Carmelite House, 50 Victoria Embankment, London EC4Y 0DZ

An Hachette UK Company
www.hachette.co.uk
www.hachettechildrens.co.uk

Keira
the Film Star Fairy

Daisy Meadows

ORCHARD

www.rainbowmagicbooks.co.uk

Contents

Story One

The Silver Script

The Silver Script

"Look, there's Julianna Stewart!" whispered Kirsty Tate, spying the film star reading her script.

"Who would have thought a famous actress would come here to Wetherbury Village?" said her best friend, Rachel Walker.

Julianna Stewart was starring in a movie called *The Starlight Chronicles*, and it was being filmed in Mrs Croft's garden! Someone from a film company had knocked on her door one day and asked if they could use her pretty cottage for the movie.

Mrs Croft was a friend of Kirsty's parents and had managed to get the girls parts as magical fairies — which was perfect for them! They had secretly visited Fairyland many

times and were always ready
to protect their fluttery friends
from mean Jack Frost and his
naughty goblin servants.

"I can't wait to try on our costumes!" grinned Kirsty.

The film set bustled with people. Helpers known as runners fetched props, and dancers practised their steps. The girls watched as Julianna took her place in front of Chad Stenning, the actor playing the fairy prince.

"And . . . action!" cried the director.

Everyone watched as Chad gave a deep bow. "Please walk with me on the terrace. There is something I must say." He offered his arm to Julianna and led her off the set.

"Excellent!" announced the director.

"I haven't seen that runner before," said Rachel, nudging her friend. "He seems in a terrible hurry."

The runner rushed past the actors, then snatched a script from the director's table.

"That's not a runner," Kirsty said breathessly, spotting a patch of green skin. "It's a goblin!"

Rachel gasped as she caught sight of a pair of warty green feet.

The girls started to follow

him just as the director called, "Action!"

Everyone waited for Julianna and Chad to start speaking. But they were totally silent.

At last Julianna spoke.

"My mind's gone blank!" she exclaimed.

"That's strange," whispered Rachel. "She's never forgotten her words before. Something – or someone – is upsetting things."

"We must find that goblin!" Kirsty replied.

Rachel
led the
way
along a
path of
stepping
stones
that
led to a
meadow
behind

Mrs Croft's cottage. It was full
of mobile homes in all shapes
and sizes. The actors and crew
were staying here together

during filming.

"That way!" cried Rachel, watching the goblin's baseball cap disappearing behind a plush-looking silver trailer.

Suddenly, a wardrobe mistress with a tape measure around her neck pushed a rail of fancy fairy outfits right across their path.

"Coming through!" she cried.

Kirsty sighed. "We'll never catch the goblin now. It'll be too late by the time we get past these costumes."

As the girls tried to step
around the rail, tiny scarlet
stars began to shimmer and fizz
above a beautiful gown until

suddenly, a pretty fairy burst out from it, landing on the rail.

"Hi!" she smiled. "I'm Keira the Film Star Fairy."

"Hello!" grinned Kirsty and Rachel, following the fairy as she fluttered to a quiet part of the meadow.

"I look after movie-makers in Fairyland and the human world," she explained. "And I really need your help."

Kirsty and Rachel listened as Keira told them about her three precious magical objects.

"The silver script makes sure the actors get their lines right. The magical megaphone helps directors organise everyone and the enchanted clapperboard gets the camera rolling. Everything was fine," she sighed, "until Jack Frost decided he wanted to be a film star."

Keira told the girls how the Ice Lord had sent his goblins to snatch the silver script.

"If we don't find it," the little fairy went on, "Julianna and the others won't be able to perform properly!"

"We just saw a goblin steal a script!" cried Kirsty, as Keira fluttered into her jacket pocket.

"This way!" said the fairy, pointing her shimmering wand towards the woods.

Kirsty peeped through the trees. "I can see the goblin!" she gasped. "He's got the silver script, and he's not alone!"

"I have to be the director!" they heard a pointy-nosed goblin shout.

"Only if I can be the prince," snapped another.

Within moments they were tugging at the script and arguing.

"I've got an idea," whispered Rachel. "Keira, would you be able to magic us some smart clothes?"

"Of course!" replied Keira, waving her wand and transforming their outfits into suits and dark glasses.

The girls stepped into the clearing.

"We're from Hollywood," Rachel announced. "And we thought you might like some tips."

A goblin with big ears shrugged his shoulders.

"Let's start with some acting exercises," began Rachel. "I'll give you a scene to act out."

"Shan't," yelled the goblin clutching the silver script.

"Oh," sighed Rachel. "But you've got the starring role!"

"I'll do it!" he cried suddenly.

"Just imagine," continued Rachel, "that you are a famous author. Now pretend you are coming to my office to deliver your new story."

"Are we ready?" cut in Kirsty suddenly. "Then . . . action!"

The goblin opened an imaginary door.

"I think you'll enjoy reading this," he began importantly, handing her the silver script.

Suddenly, Keira burst from Kirsty's pocket and tapped the silver script with her wand, shrinking it to fairy size.

"Thanks, Mr Goblin Writer!" she smiled.

The goblins squawked and leapt with rage.

"This is going back to Fairyland," she told them

firmly. "Where it belongs."

When the silly goblins had run off to hide from Jack Frost, Keira smiled.

"Thank you," she said, magically changing the girls back into their normal clothes, and disappearing in a puff of fairy dust.

"Goodbye!" waved the girls.

"Let's go back to the film set," Kirsty suggested, linking arms with her best friend. "I'll bet those rehearsals are on track again!"

Story Two

The Magical Megaphone

The Magical Megaphone

Back in Mrs Croft's garden, people scurried around everywhere. "Let's sit over there," suggested Rachel, pointing to a wooden bench. It was the perfect place to watch the rehearsal.

"Let's roll!" announced the director.

Everyone waited for Julianna to say her first line, but instead,
 she wandered over to Chad, who was still having his make-up done!

"Miss Stewart," began the director gently. "The scene with your fairy servants under the tree comes first. Then you move across to the prince."

Julianna frowned, looking very confused.

"Let's try again. Ladies-in-waiting, where are you?" he bellowed.

"Over here," they waved from across the garden. "Where you told us to be."

"That's not what I said!" he wailed.

"Something's wrong," said Kirsty. "No one knows what they should be doing!"

"This is awful!" declared Rachel as they watched the director trying to sort out the muddle.

Suddenly, the fountain in front of them began to bubble higher, and there, rising on the crest of the cascade, was Keira! The little fairy's face was pale with worry as she beckoned them over to the bushes at the back of the garden.

"Will you come with me to Fairyland?" she gasped, her eyes wide. "We haven't got much time!"

Keira explained that Queen Titania had made a special request for Kirsty and Rachel's help.

"Of course we'll come!" cried both the girls at once.

A whirl of fairy magic spun
around the friends as they
felt themselves getting smaller
and smaller. Soon they were
the same size as Keira, with
shimmering wings on their
shoulders. The three fairies

joined hands and closed their eyes. When they opened them again, they were gliding above the emerald hills of Fairyland. They landed in the pretty walled garden of the Fairyland Palace. In the centre was a pond, which Kirsty and Rachel recognised as the magical Seeing Pool. Queen Titania was standing next to it.

"Hello again, dear girls!" she said warmly.

"Your Majesty," said Rachel breathlessly.

The queen waved her wand over the Seeing Pool.

"Thank you for coming," she said sadly. "*The Starlight Chronicles* is in serious trouble."

As the pool shone with magical light, a picture of Jack Frost slowly formed on

the surface.

"He's on the film set!" gasped Rachel.

As they watched, the Ice Lord picked up a megaphone and stuffed it under his cloak.

"And that's the magical megaphone!" cried Keira. "I'd lent it to *The Starlight Chronicles* to make sure filming went well. But now it's locked away in the Ice Castle!"

Suddenly Rachel and Kirsty realised why everything had been going wrong.

"Would you all go to Jack Frost's Ice Castle to find it?" Queen Titania asked the girls.

They nodded their heads. "Of course, Your Majesty," said Kirsty.

"Thank you, dear friends," said the queen, lifting up her wand once again.

The magical megaphone should be easy to find. Its sound can travel for miles."

Queen Titania pointed her wand up to the sky. Fairy dust sparkled and flashed all around

the fairies, and when it settled,
the beautiful palace gardens
had disappeared. Instead they
found themselves in a dark
wood. A wind blew through
the icy trees, making all the
fairies shiver.

"The Ice Castle is on the other side of this wood,"

whispered Keira.

Suddenly a chilly voice rang around the trees.

"You goblins are useless!" it cried.

"That's Jack Frost!" gasped Rachel, looking nervously

around her.

"All you had to do was bring back the silver script!" the voice boomed.

The fairies flew through freezing clouds towards the Ice Castle. As they got closer, Jack Frost's angry shouts got louder and louder.

They landed in the courtyard, and the noise was terrible. Jack Frost was pacing around, shouting at the goblins through the magical megaphone!

The goblins were all wandering around with their fingers in their ears, bumping into each other in confusion and wailing at the horrible noise.

"We have to stop him," Kirsty

shouted over the din.

"I can't hear you!" Rachel frowned.

Luckily, Keira knew just what to do. She lightly tapped her wand against her ear, and as golden stars surrounded them, the girls felt a pair of earplugs slip into their ears. In blissful silence, they looked around. One by one the golden stars touched the clueless goblins, and earplugs slid into their ears too.

"Peace at last," grinned one.

 Jack Frost was ordering the goblins about, but they just stared gormlessly. They couldn't hear a word!

"Hurry up! Get on with it!" he screamed.

Jack Frost was getting more and more furious.

"What's wrong with this thing?" he snarled, shaking the megaphone and peering inside it. Rachel spotted her

chance. As quick
as a flash, she
darted inside
the other
end and then
burst out, right

into Jack Frost's face!

"Aarrghh!" he yelled
in shock, dropping the
megaphone.

"That's mine!" cried Keira,
zooming towards her precious
possession. As soon as her hand
touched it, it shrank down to
fairy size.

Kirsty and Rachel followed Keira up into the air, taking care to flutter out of Jack Frost's reach.

"Pesky fairies!" he fumed. "Come back here or I'll set my goblins on you!" The meanie glared at his servants, but they simply grunted, shrugged and scratched their heads.

"They can't hear a word!" chuckled Keira, pulling her earplugs out. The girls did the same and then all three sets of earplugs magically

disappeared.

"What a gormless bunch!" barked Jack Frost, storming up and down the courtyard. "Can't you lot do anything I tell you?"

"What's up with him?"
sniffed one of the goblins,
nudging a pal in the ribs.
The other goblin gawped at
his master then pulled a silly
face. "Lucky we've got these

earplugs in!" he sniggered.

"Time to go!" beamed Keira, pointing her wand at the girls and holding on tight to her magical megaphone. In a fizz of stars, she whisked them all away with Jack Frost's shouts still echoing in the distance.

After everyone had said goodbye, a sparkling shower of magic from Keira's wand turned Rachel and Kirsty back to human size again. Could this holiday get any more exciting?

Story Three

The Enchanted
Clapperboard

The Enchanted Clapperboard

Kirsty and Rachel were both feeling very excited. It was finally time for them to play their parts as extras in *The Starlight Chronicles*! "I can't wait to show our costumes to Keira," whispered Kirsty.

Each girl was dressed in a pale pink gown, and with all the other extras, had spent the morning having their hair and make-up done. The first scene was to be filmed inside Mrs Croft's pretty house. They would be attending the fairy princess on the morning of her wedding.

"I hope I can remember where to stand!" said an extra called Angel. Her friend, Emily, anxiously bent down to tie the ribbons on her satin slippers.

Suddenly, the door opened and there were gasps as Julianna stepped onto the set.

"You look perfect!" exclaimed Rachel.

Large dazzling spotlights shone onto the sparkling set as the director held up his special movie clapperboard.

"Quiet please," he began. "Lights, camera . . ."

The girls waited to hear the word "action", but nothing happened.

"The clapperboard is stuck," he said, frowning.

The flustered crew tried to get it working, but it refused to snap shut. An assistant ran up and passed the director two thick wooden sticks he had found in the props department.

"My camera won't work, either," said a confused camera operator.

"There's something funny going on around here," whispered Rachel.

"Look," Kirsty said quietly to her friend, pointing. "That camera's glowing!"

The girls stared as Keira whooshed out of the lens.

"Oh girls," she cried. "Jack Frost has stolen my enchanted clapperboard, and given it to his goblins!"

Rachel and Kirsty were horrified. "What does it do?" asked Rachel.

"It makes sure filming always goes to plan," Keira explained.

"That must be why it's going wrong today," guessed Kirsty.

Suddenly there was a giggle outside the door, and the sound of footsteps on the stairs.

"That sounded like a goblin," said Kirsty. "Do you think the enchanted clapperboard is here?"

"If you were fairies," said Keira, "it would be much easier to search around without being seen."

Keira waved her wand and a cascade of golden fairy dust

magically shrank them to
fairy size.

"Let's go!" said Kirsty,
swooping upstairs and
following the sound of giggling
into Mrs Croft's bedroom. Two
goblins were bouncing up and
down on the bed. One had a
clapperboard under his arm.

"That's the enchanted clapperboard!" said Keira.

"Give that back to Keira right now!" declared Rachel, fluttering forward.

The goblin was so surprised, he lost his balance and bounced off the bed with a loud crash. Then, without looking back, they both shot out of the door, still clutching the enchanted clapperboard.

At the top of the stairs, the goblins played tug-of-war with it, until suddenly one of them

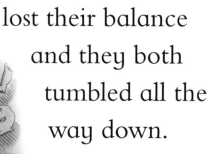

lost their balance and they both tumbled all the way down.

"Come on!" Keira cried, zooming after the goblins. "We have to stop them!"

Downstairs, a sound technician had wedged her microphone in the old ceiling beams and three runners were trying to pull it free. Half the costumes had gone missing,

and the make-up artist's
brushes had fallen through the
floorboards. The poor director
was sitting in the middle of it
all with his head in his hands.

"We have to finish filming
tonight," he muttered.
"Mrs Croft is coming back

tomorrow! Let's set up a screen and watch the rushes," he went on.

"What are the rushes?" asked Rachel as everyone sprang into action.

"They're the scenes from the day before," Keira explained. "The director always checks them to make sure nothing needs to be re-shot."

The girls watched as two runners pointed a projector at the white wall, drew the curtains and turned off the

lights. The room was soon
packed as everyone gathered
for the viewing.

Through the gloom, Kirsty
saw something move behind
the sofa.

The goblins were watching
the film scenes and scowling.
"I'd make a much better star,"

one said, tucking the enchanted clapperboard under his arm and jumping in front of the projector screen.

"No you wouldn't," squeaked the other one. "I would!"

Everyone in the room gasped.

"Quick – grab it!" cried Keira.

The three fluttering fairies reached the enchanted clapperboard a second too late.

"I don't remember filming this," said the director, frowning. The goblins began pushing

each other as the outlines of
their bodies filled the white
wall behind them.

"Who hired these naughty
extras?" he demanded. "And
where did they get those
hideous costumes?"

As the goblins shoved
and fought, the enchanted
clapperboard fell to the ground.

"This is our chance!" said
Rachel. As a runner jumped up
to chase the goblins from the
room, the three friends zipped
towards the clapperboard.
The film crew were so busy
staring at the goblins, no one
saw the little fairy land beside
the enchanted
clapperboard
and shrink it
back to fairy
size.

"I've got
it!" she cried, as

the three of them swooped out through the open window.

Just then, they heard Mrs Croft's front door open, and the goblins ran out scowling, and disappeared into the woods.

"Thanks for your help today," said Keira. "Now

filming can get back to normal."

With a swoop of her magic wand, she returned Kirsty and Rachel to their normal size.

"I'm going to take the enchanted clapperboard back to Fairyland," explained Keira. "But I've got a feeling that *The Starlight Chronicles* is going to be a sparkling success!"

With that, she disappeared in a burst of golden light.

"We're ready for you now, girls!" a runner called to them. "The cameras are working again."

Kirsty and Rachel hurried inside, just in time to hear the director say three truly magical words:

"Lights! Camera! Action!"

**If you enjoyed this story,
you may want to read**

Tamara the Tooth Fairy
Early Reader

Here's how the story begins...

"My wobbly tooth has finally fallen out!" Kirsty Tate called out to her best friend. She had arrived just that morning at Rachel Walker's house, where she was staying for part of the summer holidays.

"That's brilliant! We've never met the Tooth Fairy!" said

Rachel, as the girls changed into their pyjamas. "I wonder what she's like?"

Climbing into bed, Kirsty put her tooth safely under the pillow. "The Tooth Fairy is so quiet that she never wakes children up," Kirsty yawned.

The two friends had a very special secret. They had often visited Fairyland. Sometimes naughty Jack Frost and his goblins made terrible mischief, and the girls had often helped the fairies defeat them. Rachel

smiled and turned out the light.
It had been a long day, and the
girls were soon asleep.

When Rachel's alarm clock
went off in the morning, she
sat up and looked eagerly over
to where her best friend was
sleeping.

Kirsty opened her eyes and
lifted her pillow. "My tooth
is still here," she said in a
disappointed voice.

"The Tooth Fairy is probably
confused because you're staying
here instead of at home,"

Rachel said, jumping out of bed to comfort her friend. "I expect she'll come tonight."

"Perhaps she left a coin and forgot to take the tooth," said Kirsty, picking up the pillow and shaking it. "Or maybe the coin got stuck inside somehow?"

Read
Tamara the Tooth Fairy
Early Reader
to find out
what happens next!

Meet the first seven
Rainbow Magic Fairies

There's a fairy book for everyone at:
www.rainbowmagicbooks.co.uk

RAINBOW magic

Become a
Rainbow Magic
fairy friend and be the first to
see sneak peeks of new books.

There are lots of special offers and exclusive
competitions to win sparkly
Rainbow Magic prizes.

Sign up today at
www.rainbowmagicbooks.co.uk